1.99

The Skeleton in the Smithsonian

by Ron Roy
illustrated by Timothy Bush

A STEPPING STONE BOOK™

Random House 🏠 New York

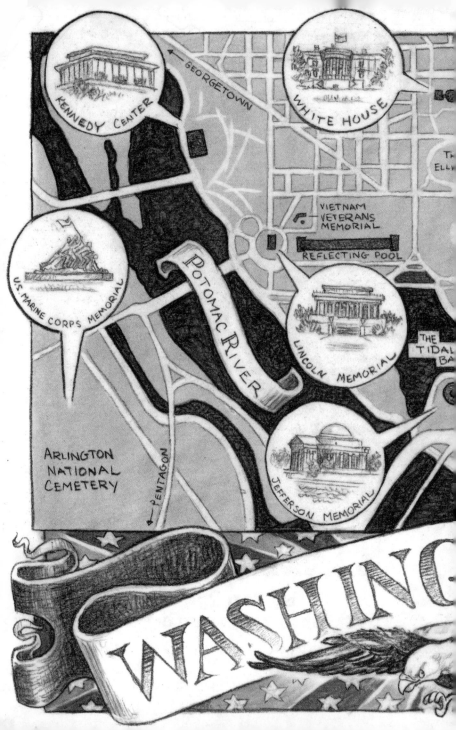

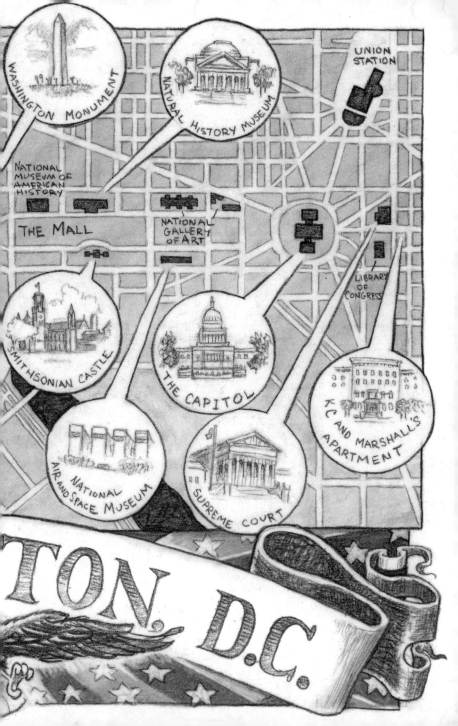

This book is dedicated to teachers everywhere.

—R.R.

Photo credits: pp. 88–89, Smithsonian Institution Archives, Record Unit 95, Box 21, Neg. #82-3196, Neg. #10192, and Box 30, Neg. #76-4354.

www.randomhouse.com/kids

Library of Congress Cataloging-in-Publication Data
Roy, Ron.
The skeleton in the Smithsonian / by Ron Roy ; illustrated by Timothy Bush.
   p.   cm. — (Capital mysteries ; #3)
"A Stepping Stone Book."
SUMMARY: When Leonard Fisher claims to be the long-lost heir to the Smithsonian fortune, KC and Marshall set out to prove that he is a phony.
ISBN 0-307-26517-X (pbk.) — ISBN 0-307-46517-9 (lib. bdg.)
[1. Smithsonian Institution—Fiction. 2. Skeletons—Fiction.
3. Washington (D.C.)—Fiction.] I. Bush, Timothy, ill. II. Title.
III. Series.
PZ7.R8139Sk 2003 [Fic]—dc21   2002154480

Printed in the United States of America
First Edition   10 9 8 7 6 5 4 3 2 1

Contents

1

Pizza with the President

"Why do I have to watch a bunch of disgusting bugs eat their supper?" KC asked. She and Marshall were in the O. Orkin Insect Zoo at the National Museum of Natural History.

"Because," Marshall explained, "Spike has stopped eating, and I want to find out why." Spike was Marshall's pet tarantula. Marshall was crazy about anything with more than four legs.

"Okay, okay," KC said. "But we can only stay for a few minutes. We have to be at the White House at five-thirty."

They passed a beehive behind glass,

then an African termite mound. Some little kids were petting a huge cockroach held by a museum scientist. KC unzipped her backpack, pulled out her camera, and snapped a picture.

Marshall headed right for the tarantulas. A woman was dropping food into a glass-sided container. About ten people were watching. Marshall wriggled his way to the front. He saw two tarantulas pounce on the food. The black spiders were the size of Marshall's hands.

"Gross," KC muttered.

"My tarantula isn't eating," Marshall told the woman. "What can I do?"

"What have you been feeding it?" the woman asked.

"Mostly flies," Marshall said. "And crickets, when I can find them."

"It may be bored with that food," the woman said. "Tarantulas like variety." She put her hand on the tarantula tank. "These guys get beetles, grubs, crickets, cockroaches, moths, and other insects." The woman wrote something on a piece of paper and handed it to Marshall. "Try this place in Florida. They sell live insects online," she said. "They'll send them right to your door."

Marshall thanked the woman. "Good luck," she called as he and KC walked toward the exit.

"Well, that was just super," KC said in the elevator. "I may *never* eat again."

Marshall grinned. "Spiders have to live, too," he said. "What would the world be like without them?"

"Much better!" KC said. She gave him

a friendly bump with her shoulder.

Marshall returned the nudge as the elevator door opened. When they reached the exit, a family of tourists was staggering in. "It must be a hundred degrees out there," the woman said, wiping her face with a hankie. The man smiled when he felt the air-conditioning.

"I wanna see the bugs!" their little boy said.

KC and Marshall stepped out into the heat. It was five o'clock, but the sun was still beating down on Washington.

A red-faced man in shorts walked up to the museum's entrance. "Hope you're not planning to go to the Smithsonian Castle," he said to KC and Marshall. He tilted his head toward the red building across the Mall lawn. "The hottest day of the year and the air-conditioning breaks down!"

KC glanced over at the stone building that looked like a castle. A stream of people hurried outside. Two guards stood at the exit, making sure everyone left. Near the entrance was parked a white van with ACE AIR-CONDITIONING on the side.

"They sure don't look happy," KC said as they headed for Pennsylvania Avenue. President Zachary Thornton was waiting for them at the White House. Ever since KC and Marshall had saved him from evil scientists, he'd been their friend.

"Is your mom coming tonight, too?" Marshall asked KC.

She nodded. "The president is sending a car to pick her up at work."

Marshall smiled at KC. "President Thornton really likes her."

KC blushed. "So? They just hang out together," she said.

Marshall rolled his eyes. "KC, you and I hang out together. When adults hang out, it's called dating," he said.

KC was quiet for the rest of the walk to the White House.

They went to the special entrance where a marine guard stood on duty. He smiled when he saw the kids.

"Hi, KC. Hi, Marshall," the marine said. "The president is expecting you."

"Hi, Arnold," KC said. "We're having pizza with him and my mom."

The marine winked. "Yeah, I know. She got here a little while ago. I think the president is sweet on her."

"Told you," Marshall said to KC.

"It's not serious!" KC insisted.

They followed Arnold to the president's private apartment. Arnold rapped on the door and a voice said, "Come in."

The president and KC's mom were seated at a table, drinking lemonade. President Thornton was setting up a Monopoly board. His fluffy cat, George, was purring on his lap. "Hi, KC. Hi, Marshall," he said. "Have some lemonade. You look hot."

"It's roasting out there," Marshall said. "And guess what? The air-conditioning broke in the Smithsonian building."

"The Castle?" the president asked. "They'll get it fixed by tomorrow, I'm sure."

KC gave her mom a kiss. "Where's the pizza?" she asked.

"The cook's making it right now," KC's mom said. She looked across at the president. "What is he putting on it, Zachary?"

KC couldn't get used to hearing her mom call the President of the United States by his first name. KC called him sir or Mr. President.

The president grinned. "Rat tails and toad tongues," he said.

The vice president, Mary Kincaid, walked into the room. She said hello, then handed the president a folded piece of paper. "I hope this is a gag, sir."

President Thornton quickly read what was on the paper. When he looked up, his grin was gone. "Someone is claiming to be the heir to James Smithson," he said.

"Who's James Smithson?" KC asked.

"He was the man who started the Smithsonian Institution," the president said. "He was a wealthy British scientist who died in the 1800s. Mr. Smithson left his money to his nephew, about half a million dollars. Smithson's will stated that if the nephew died without children, the money should come to the United States to create the Smithsonian Institution."

The president scooted George off his lap and walked to a shelf. He pulled out a book and opened it to a picture of James Smithson. "When the nephew died without heirs," President Thornton went on, "Congress received the money and the Smithsonian Castle was begun in 1847. Since then, many other buildings have been added."

"And now someone is claiming to be an heir?" KC's mom asked. "So that half a million dollars . . ."

"That's right." The president glanced down at the note. "This man—Leonard Fisher—claims that the money used to start the Smithsonian Institution really belongs to him. And with interest, it would be worth millions of dollars!"

Everyone stared at the president. "Can he do that?" KC asked.

"He can say whatever he wants," the president said. He turned to the vice president. "Mary, I'd like to meet with Mr. Fisher tonight, if possible."

A man in a white jacket entered the room carrying a pizza. "Put it next to the Monopoly board, please," the president said. Then he picked up the dice. "Since I'm the president," he said, "I get to roll first."

2

The Unknown Heir

KC and Marshall were clearing up the pizza plates when Leonard Fisher and his attorney were announced.

"We appreciate your coming on such short notice," the president told the two men.

"No problem," Mr. A. C. Rook, the attorney, said. He smiled, showing a row of small, sharp teeth.

Leonard Fisher sat down on a couch. He wore a blue jacket over a white shirt with no tie. "Thanks for inviting us," he said. "I want to get this settled so I can get back to work soon."

"Oh, what do you do, Mr. Fisher?" Mary Kincaid asked.

"I'm a landscape designer," he said. "When rich people want a nice garden, they call me."

Just then Mr. Fisher sneezed. Grabbing a paper napkin, he wiped his eyes and nose. "Sorry, I'm allergic to those." He pointed to a blue vase of flowers on the table.

"You're allergic to flowers?" Mary Kincaid asked.

"Just those tall ones, the lilies," Mr. Fisher said.

Mary Kincaid made a phone call. A few seconds later, a maid came and removed the vase.

"Well, why don't we get started?" Rook said. "You've read Mr. Fisher's claim.

Have you any questions, Mr. President?"

"Yes, I do," the president said. "Mr. Fisher claims to be James Smithson's heir. Can you tell us, Mr. Fisher, just how you are related to him?"

Leonard Fisher nodded. "Sure. James Smithson left his money to his nephew, Henry Hungerford. What no one knows is that Hungerford had a child. A son. He was my great-great-grandfather. When Hungerford died, the money came to the United States." Mr. Fisher tapped himself on the chest. "That money should be mine."

"But it's always been thought that Mr. Hungerford died without getting married or having children," Mary Kincaid said. "That's why the money came to the United States."

Mr. Fisher shrugged. "I guess everyone thought wrong," he said. He glanced at his lawyer.

The lawyer pulled a thick document from his briefcase. He placed it on the table. "These papers prove our claim," Rook said, showing his teeth. "A direct line from Henry Hungerford to my client."

"May I ask why you waited until now to come forward?" Mary Kincaid asked as she picked up the stapled pages.

"My client only learned about his connection to Hungerford recently," Rook explained.

Mary Kincaid glanced at the first page, then passed the document to the president. "Our lawyers will need some time to look these over," she said. "Naturally, the documents have to be examined very carefully. We need to be sure Mr. Fisher really is related to James Smithson. We may require more than a few sheets of paper."

"What other proof do you need?" the lawyer asked. "Mr. Fisher is directly related to James Smithson through Smithson's nephew."

"Our attorneys will decide that," said the president. "No one wants to cheat Mr. Fisher out of what is rightfully his."

The adults looked at each other.

"Um, how about DNA?" Marshall asked.

Everyone turned to look at him. Except KC. She was watching Mr. Fisher. He had a funny smile on his face.

Marshall blushed and took a sip of his lemonade.

"Well, I was thinking, why not compare James Smithson's DNA with Mr. Fisher's?" he asked. "If they're related, the DNA will prove it."

Mr. Fisher smiled at Marshall. "That's a good idea," he said, "except for one thing. We don't have any of James Smithson's DNA."

"Yes, we do!" KC said. She pointed through a window. "His body is in the Smithsonian Castle."

"It is?" the lawyer asked.

"Yes," the president said. "Smithson's remains are in a sarcophagus on permanent display there."

"Then that's perfect," the lawyer said, beaming at Leonard Fisher. "My client will be glad to have the tests whenever you want."

President Thornton was quiet for a moment. Then he stood up. "Right. We'll open the crypt to take a DNA sample from James Smithson," he said. "Mary, will you ask my secretary to arrange that for tomorrow?"

Mary Kincaid nodded. "Yes, sir."

Rook snapped his briefcase shut. "My client is staying at the Dupont Inn," he said. "We'll wait to hear from you."

Mary Kincaid stood up. "Thank you, gentlemen," she said, walking them to the door. "Someone will contact Mr. Fisher for his DNA sample."

After Mr. Fisher and his lawyer had gone, the president looked wearily at KC and Marshall. "If Mr. Fisher is Henry Hungerford's heir, the United States may lose the Smithsonian."

"Maybe the DNA won't match," said Marshall.

"You're right, Marshall," the president said, straightening up. "We should keep a positive attitude. Anyway, we'll know one way or the other after we open that sarcophagus tomorrow."

"Can we watch?" KC asked.

The president gave KC and Marshall a sly look. "Have you ever seen a hundred-and-seventy-year-old skeleton?"

3
Spying and Lying

"At least the air-conditioning is working again," KC whispered to Marshall. They were in the Smithsonian Castle with the president and two scientists. It was only nine o'clock in the morning, so the building wasn't open to the public yet.

"Why are you whispering?" Marshall asked with a grin. "Scared of ghosts?"

"You two are about to witness history," the president broke in. "Without that gift from James Smithson, Washington, D.C., would be a different place."

"All set, Mr. President," one of the scientists said. "This should only take a few minutes." She was wearing rubber gloves and carried a specimen jar.

They were in the main room of the Castle. To the left was another, smaller room. Through the open arch, KC could see a gray casket resting on a stone pedestal. The president entered the room first, and the others followed.

The marble sarcophagus stood in the center of the room. There was no other furniture. A small sign told the public that inside the casket were the remains of James Smithson, who died in 1829.

KC felt herself trembling. She hoped Marshall wouldn't notice.

"Okay, let's do it," President Thornton said, moving back to stand next to KC and Marshall. His voice sounded hollow in the quiet room. They watched one scientist insert the flat end of a crowbar into the crack under the sarcophagus lid. Then both scientists leaned on the bar until the lid was raised high enough for them to get their hands beneath it. They carefully removed the lid and set it aside.

The president put his hands on KC's and Marshall's shoulders. "Come meet James Smithson," he said quietly.

The kids stepped forward. KC felt as if she were in a spooky movie. She expected to see a fully preserved body, wrapped like a mummy. But lying on the bottom of the casket were only bones and bits of clothing. Long gray hair still covered part of the skull.

The female scientist reached in while her partner held the open jar. She removed a few hairs from the skull and dropped them into the container. Then she turned and looked at the president. "Anything else, sir?" she asked.

"That's all you need?" he asked. "A few hairs?"

The scientist smiled. "That's all we need."

"When will we know?" the president asked. "I hate to rush you, but we need an answer as soon as possible."

"We have our best people working on this," the scientist said. "In a couple of hours we'll be able to tell how these samples compare with Mr. Fisher's hair."

President Thornton smiled. "Thank you."

The scientists replaced the sarcophagus lid, sealed the specimen jar, and left the building.

The president said good-bye to the kids on the front steps of the Castle. KC and Marshall watched him step into his waiting car. When it pulled away, they began walking home.

"So if Mr. Fisher is telling the truth, he'll be a zillionaire by tomorrow," said Marshall.

KC and Marshall headed toward the Capitol. When they passed a large garden, KC took her camera out of her backpack. She snapped a picture of Marshall in front of some white blossoms covered with monarch butterflies.

KC studied one of the blossoms. "That's funny," she said.

"What's funny?" Marshall asked. He was watching a fat yellow bee.

"The sign says these are lilies," KC told

him. "Remember when Leonard Fisher sneezed yesterday? He said he was allergic to the lilies in the vase. But the flowers in the vase didn't look anything like these."

"So maybe he was allergic to some other flower," Marshall said.

"I think gardeners should know one flower from another," KC said as they walked.

She gave Marshall a sideways look. "Another thing," KC added. "Did you notice the look on Mr. Fisher's face when you mentioned DNA?"

"No," Marshall said.

"Well, I was watching him," KC said. "When you brought up DNA, he got all smiley."

Marshall laughed. "Wouldn't you be

happy if you found out you could inherit a lot of money?"

KC shook her head. "It wasn't that kind of smile, Marsh. It was sneaky, like the way you smile when you're cheating at Monopoly."

"I don't cheat!" Marshall said.

KC grinned. "Yeah, and that hundred-dollar bill just happened to stick to your elbow last night."

A few minutes later, they were waiting for a light across the street from the Dupont Inn. "Isn't that where Mr. Fisher said he was staying?" KC asked.

"I think so," Marshall said. "Why?"

KC pushed the button for the WALK sign so they could cross. "We should spy on him."

"KC, the president can take care of this

Smithsonian stuff," Marshall said. "He doesn't need you."

KC took Marshall by the arm. "Let's at least see if Fisher is there."

The kids passed through a revolving door into the hotel.

The lobby was decorated to look like a tropical island. There were palm trees in big pots, and pictures of sandy beaches hanging on the walls. Soft music came from hidden speakers.

KC walked up to the desk. A tall man stood behind it typing on a computer. "Excuse me," KC said. "My friend is feeling faint from the heat. Could he have something to drink?"

"No problem." The man pointed to a small table. "There are drinks and pastries over there. Help yourself."

"Thank you," KC said. She turned away, then spun back. "By the way, is Mr. Fisher in?"

"Mr. Leonard Fisher, the musician?" the clerk asked. "Yes, he went up about ten minutes ago."

KC stared at him. "Musician? I thought he was a gardener," she said. "Are there *two* Leonard Fishers staying here?"

"I don't think so." The man tapped a few keys on his computer. "No, it's showing only one Leonard Fisher. I was here when he checked in. He was carrying a long black case. When I asked about it, he said he played in a band. Would you like me to ring Mr. Fisher in his room?"

"Oh, no, thank you," KC said. "We'll just wait. We want to surprise him."

"Suit yourself," the clerk said.

KC sighed and sat in an armchair where she could watch the elevators. "Gardener, musician. Marsh, there's something very weird going on," she said.

Marshall bit into a jelly doughnut and relaxed in the air-conditioned lobby. "I know someone who has an overactive imagination," he said. He wiggled deeper into his chair. "I wonder how much a room costs in this place."

"A lot more than you have," KC said. "Unless you use some of that Monopoly money you stole."

"I didn't steal any—"

"Shhh! There he is!" KC said. She ducked behind a tree as Leonard Fisher stepped out of the elevator. He was wearing shorts, sneakers, and a light blue shirt. He was also carrying a black instrument case. The case was as tall as KC and had a handle on the side.

KC and Marshall watched Leonard Fisher cross the lobby and walk outside.

KC counted to five, then stood up. "Come on, Marshall," she whispered. "Don't let him see you!"

KC and Marshall followed Leonard Fisher. When he stopped to buy a newspaper, they hid behind a Dumpster. When he looked in a window at some clothing, they slipped into an alley.

"I feel like a jerk," Marshall said. "Tell me again why we're following this guy?"

"Because I don't trust him," KC said.

Marshall snorted. "You don't trust him? You don't *know* him, KC."

Before KC could respond, Fisher continued walking.

KC and Marshall followed.

"Can you read what it says on the back of his shirt?" KC asked.

Marshall squinted. "Um, I think it says CENTIPEDE something."

KC squinted, too. "No, I think it says CELLOPHANE something."

"Maybe it says CELLO PLAYER," Marshall tried.

Just then Fisher stopped again. He set the black case on the ground and bent down and tied his sneaker lace.

KC whipped out her camera and snapped a picture. She heard a whirring sound and realized that she had just used the last frame. She popped out the roll and put it in her pocket.

When KC looked up again, Leonard Fisher had disappeared.

"Where did he go?" she asked, turning to look all around her. There were plenty of people carrying briefcases, shopping bags, and pocketbooks. But KC saw no one with a musician's case.

"Maybe he went down there," Marshall said. A few yards away, a ramp sloped down to an underground parking garage.

"Let's look," KC said, already walking down the ramp.

The underground garage was quiet and dark. Hundreds of cars, vans, and small trucks were parked in lines. KC smelled gasoline, dust, and dampness.

"Do you see him?" she whispered, peering into the dim corners.

"Um, can we go?" Marshall asked. "This place is creeping me out."

"Yeah, okay," KC said. They walked

back up the ramp into daylight. KC realized that she had goose bumps on her arms.

"I want to drop my film off and buy another roll," she told Marshall. "And when we get home, we're going to play Monopoly again. And this time, don't cheat!"

"I don't have to cheat," Marshall said, tapping the side of his head. "I'm a better player than you."

KC chased him all the way to their building.

4
The Cemetery Bus

The next morning, KC and Marshall took a few shortcuts and reached the camera shop in ten minutes.

KC paid, then opened the cardboard packet that held the pictures and negatives. Marshall looked over her shoulder. There were pictures of KC's kittens, one of Marshall in the garden, and one of the kids petting a cockroach in the Museum of Natural History.

"Here he is," KC said. In the snapshot, Leonard Fisher was bending over to tie his sneaker lace. Next to him rested the black instrument case.

"Before we lost him," Marshall said.

The picture showed the back of Fisher's shirt, but the words printed there weren't clear enough to read. "CELERY something something," KC muttered.

"Wait a sec, I have an idea," Marshall said.

He turned to the clerk. "Can you make this picture bigger?"

"Sure, but it would cost six dollars and take about a week," the clerk said. "I'd have to send it out."

She reached under the counter and pulled out a magnifying glass. "Here, try this," she suggested.

"Thanks a lot!" KC said. She placed the round magnifying glass over the picture of Leonard Fisher. The words on his shirt were suddenly clear.

"CEMETERY STAFF, BOWIE, MARYLAND," Marshall read out loud. He and KC stared at each other.

"Cemetery staff?" KC said. "He told us he made gardens for rich people!"

KC slid the pictures back into the packet. She tucked it into her backpack and headed for the door.

Marshall thanked the clerk and followed KC. "Why would the guy lie about his job?" he asked.

"I don't know," KC said, "but it can't be good."

"What would your mom say if she heard you say that?" Marshall asked.

KC started humming over Marshall's voice.

"She'd say, 'Katherine Christine, don't jump to conclusions!'" Marshall trilled.

He sounded a lot like KC's mom.

KC stopped and looked at Marshall. "Marsh, don't you think it's weird that Leonard Fisher told the president he was a gardener but told the hotel guy he was a musician?" she asked. "And what's up with that shirt?"

"Just because his shirt has CEME-TERY written on it doesn't mean he's lying," Marshall said. "I have a shirt with a picture of a beetle on the back, but I'm not an insect."

"Says who?" KC asked, walking faster.

"Very funny," Marshall said. "And where are we going?"

"Back to the Dupont Inn."

"Oh, brother," Marshall muttered under his breath.

"Don't worry," KC said. "All I want to

do is ask him whether he's a gardener, a musician, or a gravedigger."

Marshall hooted.

"And don't tell me he has three jobs," KC said.

When they walked into the lobby, the same clerk was behind the counter. "Back for another breakfast?" he asked, raising an eyebrow.

"No, thank you," KC said. She gave him her brightest smile. "We need to talk to Leonard Fisher."

The man shook his head. "I'm afraid that's not possible. Mr. Fisher is gone for the day."

"Where did he go?" KC asked.

The clerk sighed. "Miss, I can't give out that kind of information," he said. "Now if you'll excuse me, I—"

"Probably gone home to Bowie, Maryland, right?" Marshall asked.

"That would be my guess," the man said. His phone rang and he picked it up. He turned his back on KC and Marshall.

They walked back out through the revolving doors. "Pretty clever, Marsh," KC said.

"No problem," Marshall said.

KC unzipped her pack and counted her money. "I think I have enough," she said.

"For what?" Marshall asked.

"Two bus fares."

"Uh-oh," Marshall muttered. "I have a feeling I know where we're going."

KC led Marshall toward a bus stop. "If your feeling is Bowie, Maryland, you're right," she said.

"But that's . . . that's three towns away!" said Marshall.

A man in a white shirt and necktie was sitting on the bench reading a newspaper. The headline said HEAT WAVE STRANGLES D.C.

"Excuse me, do you know which bus goes to Bowie, Maryland?" KC asked him.

"I think you want the number thirteen," he said, pulling a bus schedule out of his pocket. He studied the schedule for a moment, then folded it back up. "Yes, thirteen is the one. It should be here in a few minutes."

"So how do we find Leonard Fisher when we get there?" Marshall asked KC.

KC hadn't thought that far ahead, but she was saved from having to answer Marshall. A silver bus with a 13 in the

front window rolled to a stop. They climbed aboard the nearly empty bus. KC paid the driver, and she and Marshall took the seat right behind him.

"At least it's air-conditioned," Marshall said as the bus pulled back into the traffic and headed east.

KC inched up to talk to the driver. "Excuse me, is Bowie a big town?"

The bus driver shook his head. "It's a pretty small place," he said, turning down his radio. "What takes you there?"

"We're looking for someone," KC said. "He's a . . . a friend. We want to surprise him, but we don't know where he works. He's either a gardener or a musician."

Marshall sank lower into his seat. "Or a gravedigger," he murmured just loudly enough for KC to hear.

"Oh yeah," KC told the driver. "He might work at a cemetery."

"Well, there's only one cemetery in Bowie," the driver said. "We pass it just before we get downtown." He looked up into his mirror. "So do you want to go into town, or should I drop you off at the cemetery?"

KC swallowed. "At the cemetery, please."

5
Caught in the Act

KC sat back and hummed along with the music coming from the radio. She knew Marshall was looking at her, so she hummed louder.

"Why do I hang out with you?" Marshall asked.

KC knew he didn't expect an answer, so she didn't give him one.

"Wow!" The bus driver leaned forward and turned up the radio. "Did you hear that?" he said.

The music had stopped, and a reporter with a very smooth voice was speaking: *"According to White House officials, it has been determined that Leonard Fisher is a direct relative of James Smithson. Smithson is the man whose money started the Smithsonian Institution over one hundred and fifty years ago. Today, Fisher's DNA was compared with Smithson's. It was a definite match. Fisher's claim that the Smithsonian fortune is his seems to be true."*

KC leaned forward as far as she could. Then she heard a different voice.

"As Mr. Leonard Fisher's attorney, I can state that he is very happy that his claim is being honored. But he has no intention of taking over the Smithsonian. He will settle for one hundred million dollars, only a fraction of the total worth of all the Smithsonian buildings and their contents."

The reporter took over again. *"White House officials will comment later today. Stay tuned for more on this modern rags-to-riches story of a common man who became a multimillionaire!"*

"Imagine, a hundred million smackers!" said the driver.

"Well, that's it," Marshall said to KC. "Leonard Fisher really is related to James Smithson."

"But then why was he lying about his job?" KC insisted.

Marshall sighed. "KC, we don't know if he was," he said. "It's possible that he *is* a gardener and a musician and he works for a cemetery."

KC wasn't satisfied with that answer. She looked out the window and let her mind wander back to when she'd first met

Fisher, in the White House. Something about him still bothered her.

The bus driver's voice broke into KC's thoughts. "The cemetery's just ahead on the left," he said. Glancing into his rearview mirror, he added, "You sure you want me to leave you here?"

"Yes!" KC said.

"What time will the bus come by again?" Marshall asked.

"I go back to D.C. in ten minutes," the driver said. "But I make the same trip again in about an hour. If you're waiting here, I'll pick you up."

"We'll be here!" Marshall told him.

The driver flashed his left-turn signal and pulled over. "Have a nice time," he joked as the door swooshed open. "And good luck finding your friend."

"Thanks a lot," KC said. She and Marshall got off the bus. The driver waved and pulled back onto the road. In a minute the bus had disappeared around a corner.

The kids were standing in the grass on the side of a road. There were no buildings nearby. The road into the cemetery passed through a gate attached to two stone pillars. One of the pillars held a sign that said:

BOWIE CEMETERY
VISITING HOURS:
DAWN TO DUSK

"Come on," KC said. "Let's see if Leonard Fisher is in there."

They walked through the open gate. Birds were calling to each other in the pine trees. Fresh flowers had been placed

near several of the graves. The grass was neatly cut and the bushes seemed well taken care of.

Marshall looked at his watch. "We have to be back at the gate in fifty-six minutes."

KC laughed. "Don't worry, we will," she said.

A blue car was parked at the edge of the road. KC watched a woman take a box of flowers and some gardening tools out of the trunk. A small white dog ran around on the grass, looking as if it wanted to play.

The woman noticed the kids and waved. "Beautiful day!" she chirped.

"Is your dog friendly?" Marshall asked.

"Too friendly sometimes! Happy, come to Mommy," the woman called.

The dog went scampering over. His

owner scooped him off the ground, walked over to Marshall, and thrust the dog into his arms. "His name is Happy." Happy licked Marshall's face and wriggled with joy.

"Do you know someone named Leonard Fisher?" KC asked the woman.

The woman thought for a moment. "Hmmm, Fisher, Fisher," she said. "I don't think so. When did Mr. Fisher pass away?"

Marshall snorted.

KC gave him a poke with her elbow. "He's still alive," she said. "I think he may work here."

The woman smiled. "Then I definitely don't know him. I'm from out of town, just doing some planting on Aunt Lucy's grave."

"Thanks anyway," KC said.

Marshall set Happy on the ground, and he and KC continued to follow the road as it curved into the cemetery.

Behind them KC heard the woman say, "No, Happy, stay here with Mommy. You can't play with those children!"

Marshall grinned slyly. "'Mommy'?" he whispered. He and KC cracked up.

Just then they saw a white van driving slowly down the road. It stopped about thirty feet from where KC and Marshall were standing.

A man in jeans, a baseball cap, and sunglasses climbed out of the van. Around his waist he wore a wide leather tool belt. He reached into the van, pulled out some hedge clippers, and tucked them into one of the loops on his belt. Then he removed his hat and glasses and wiped his face on his sleeve. On the back of his shirt were the words CEMETERY STAFF, BOWIE, MARYLAND.

When he turned around, KC gasped. The man was Leonard Fisher!

6
Creepy Crypt

Leonard Fisher walked to the rear of his van, opened the door, and dragged out a lawn mower. KC heard him grunt as he lowered the machine to the ground.

Fisher reached back in and pulled out a red gas can. He unscrewed the cap from the mower's gas tank and poured in the gas. After recapping the tank, he yanked a few times on the mower's starter cord. The engine sputtered, then roared to life.

"He's a lawn guy!" Marshall whispered from their hiding spot. When they'd realized who the man was, they'd scooted behind some trees.

"Told you he lied," KC mumbled.

They watched Fisher mow the grass around a few shrubs and tombstones. He kept looking over his shoulder, as if he suspected someone was watching him.

KC and Marshall lay flat on the fallen pine needles under a large tree to make themselves less noticeable.

Leonard Fisher brought the mower back to his van, then let the engine die. He yanked the hedge clippers from his belt and walked over to some bushes next to a small stone building. He started to prune the bushes, stopping every few snips to look over his shoulder. Then he stopped cutting and stuck the clippers back into his belt. He walked quickly over to the van and opened the side door.

What he took out this time made KC

grab Marshall's arm. It was the black instrument case! Fisher held the case by the handle on its side, then nudged the van door shut with his shoulder.

As still as statues, KC and Marshall watched Fisher carry the case away from the van. He returned to the small building. To KC, it looked like a stone cottage from a fairy tale. Leonard Fisher set the case down and pulled a key ring from his pocket.

"What's he doing? Can you see?" KC whispered. A bush partly blocked her view.

Marshall stretched out until he could see better. "He's unlocking that little house," he said. "He's going inside!"

KC got up on her knees. "Come on!" she whispered.

Crouching, the kids scooted over and hid next to the white van. When KC looked through the window, she saw a square plastic sign on the front seat.

She poked Marshall and pointed at the sign: ACE AIR-CONDITIONING. "This van was in front of the Smithsonian Castle the other day!" she whispered.

KC and Marshall tiptoed on the freshly cut grass to the side of the little building. The walls were smooth gray stone, and the sloping roof was slate.

KC peeked around the building's corner. The structure had been built partly underground. The door was open wide, and two stone steps led down to the inside.

A small brass plate was fastened to the outside. In faded letters it said HERE

LIE HOMER AND ESTHER FISHER, IN ETERNAL REST.

KC gulped. This was a crypt, where cemeteries put people's coffins instead of burying them. She looked at Marshall to see if he'd figured it out.

His eyes were huge and his face had turned gray.

Holding her breath, KC moved to the front of the crypt. Marshall had his hand on her back. His hand was trembling.

There was no light in the stone building, but KC could see Leonard Fisher kneeling with his back to the door. There were two stone coffins in the crypt, one on each side of where Fisher knelt. One of the coffins was closed. The other was not. Its lid was off and leaning against the wall.

On the floor next to Fisher's knees was

the instrument case. It was open. Fisher had tossed his tool belt and the clippers into the top half.

But it was the bottom half of the case that grabbed KC's attention. In it, on blue velvet lining, lay a small skeleton.

Suddenly KC felt Marshall stumble into her. She put out her hands to stop herself from falling.

Leonard Fisher wheeled around. When he saw the kids, his mouth opened in surprise. KC watched him trying to figure out where he'd seen them before.

Then he grinned. "Well, hello," he said. "What are *you* doing here?" As he spoke, his right hand slowly moved to the instrument case. With one quick motion, he flipped it shut.

"We followed you!" KC said.

Fisher was still grinning, but his eyes looked nervous.

"You followed me? Why?"

"Because you lied to the president!" Marshall said.

Fisher shook his head. "I lied? About what?"

Before KC could answer him, Fisher jumped forward as fast as a rattlesnake strikes. He grabbed her and Marshall by the wrists and pulled them into the crypt. "Let's keep this private, shall we?" he said, releasing their hands. "Besides, it's cooler in here."

He leaned against the wall by the door. It was still open, letting sunlight into the damp chamber.

Fisher took a pack of gum from one of his pockets and held it out to the kids.

Neither took any. Fisher shrugged, slid out a piece, and began unwrapping it. "Now, you were saying . . . ?"

"You told the president you were some fancy gardener, but you really work in a cemetery," KC said.

She pointed to the instrument case. "And there's a skeleton in there. I saw it!"

Suddenly Marshall understood. "You switched skeletons!" he cried. "You're not related to James Smithson! You knew they'd check his DNA, so you put one of your dead relatives in the sarcophagus!" Marshall pointed to the open coffin. "It was him, wasn't it?"

"You're pretty smart kids," Fisher said. "Yeah, I switched. The one I left in the museum is my great-great-grandfather." He nodded toward the instrument case.

"And that's James Smithson. But by the time anyone figures that out, I'll be long gone—with a hundred million bucks in my pocket. I'll disappear forever."

"No, you won't!" KC said. "We're telling the president as soon as we get back!"

Fisher laughed. "Back? You're not going back," he said. "At least not till I'm far away from here."

He ran up the steps and out of the crypt. Before KC or Marshall could react, he'd slammed the door.

7
Trapped!

"Stop!" Marshall yelled. He leaped toward the door but tripped on KC's feet. They both fell over, then scrambled up and tried to force the metal door open. It stayed solidly shut.

"He locked it," Marshall said. "What are we gonna do?"

It was totally dark. KC couldn't even see Marshall, though she knew he was standing right next to her. "I'm sitting down," she said, "so we don't trip over each other again."

She hunched down, and she felt Marshall sit next to her. The floor of the crypt was cold, damp stone. KC felt goose bumps racing up her arms.

"Someone will come looking for us," she said. She tried to sound calm.

"Like who?" Marshall said, sounding not at all calm. "No one knows where we are!"

KC realized Marshall was right. They'd taken the number 13 bus without going home, so KC hadn't left a note for her mother. And the president had no idea where they were.

KC started to say that as soon as their parents got worried, they'd come looking. But of course, they wouldn't know where to look. Not even the FBI would find KC and Marshall in a Maryland cemetery.

Then KC remembered the one person who did know where they were.

"The bus driver!" she said. "He said he'd look for us at the gate in an hour. How much time is left, Marsh?"

The hands on Marshall's watch glowed in the dark. "He dropped us off thirty-two minutes ago," he said.

"Okay, so when we don't show up in a half hour, the bus driver will tell somebody we're in the cemetery."

"But, KC, he doesn't know that we're locked in this dumb crypt," Marshall said. "Even if someone comes to the cemetery, they won't know where to look for us!"

"Oh," KC said. She thought for a minute. "There might be more people visiting graves," she said. "We have to make a lot of loud noise. Did you see anything we can bang with?"

"Like what, a drum?" Marshall wisecracked. "KC, this is where they keep dead people. There's nothing in here but two coffins that weigh about a million pounds each."

"And the musician's case," KC said. "Could we use that?"

"I'm not touching that thing," Marshall said. "Did you forget it's filled with bones?"

"Not just bones," KC said. "I saw the hedge clippers in there, too!"

She scrambled over Marshall's knees and crawled around until she felt the instrument case. Her fingers unhooked the clasps, and she lifted the lid. She took a deep breath and reached in, knowing the skeleton was lying there. But her fingers felt the rubber handles of the hedge clippers. They'd fallen on top of the bones when Fisher slammed the case shut.

KC grabbed the heavy clippers and crawled back to Marshall.

"Did you get 'em?" he asked.

"Yes!" KC began banging on the crypt door with the metal blades. The clanging noise bounced around the space.

"I hope it sounds that loud outside," Marshall said.

KC smacked the tool against the door until her arms grew tired, and then Marshall took over.

When Marshall stopped, KC heard a high-pitched noise outside. "Do you hear that?" she asked.

"It's Happy!" Marshall cried. "He's barking! He knows we're in here!"

Marshall dropped the hedge clippers and began yelling. KC and Marshall could

hear the little dog's excited yelping. He sounded close.

"Good dog, Happy!" Marshall yelled. "Happy, go get Mommy! Find Mommy!"

Happy stopped barking. KC and Marshall pressed their ears against the door. Then they heard a wonderful sound. "Is someone in there?" Happy's owner asked.

"Yes!" Marshall screamed.

"Can you get us out?" KC cried.

"There's a big padlock," the woman said. "I can't imagine how I'll get it unlocked."

Happy began to bark again.

"I know!" the woman yelled through the door. "I passed a gas station when I drove here. I'll go there and get someone to break this lock. Will you be all right?"

"We'll be okay," KC said. "But please hurry!"

After she left, the kids slumped back onto the stone floor. The floor was cold, and KC shivered.

"It's f-freezing in this place," Marshall said, shivering. "I'll never complain about the heat again!"

The kids sat, leaning against each other for warmth. KC felt herself growing sleepy. Her eyes closed, but she blinked them open again. Her head felt so heavy. She let her chin fall and closed her eyes. This time she didn't try to open them again.

The next thing she knew, Marshall was shaking her by the shoulder. "KC, wake up! They're here!" he cried.

8
Found

When KC sat up, she felt groggy. She heard a man's voice through the door. "Are you kids all right?" the voice called.

"We're okay!" Marshall yelled back.

"Great, we'll have you out in a jiffy," the voice said. "Stand back while I bust this lock!"

KC and Marshall moved a few feet away from the door. Suddenly they heard a loud smashing sound of metal against metal. The door opened, and sunlight flooded the crypt. Blinking in the sudden light, KC and Marshall staggered up the steps.

The first thing KC saw was Happy, the little white dog. He was straining at his leash, barking and practically dancing with excitement.

Happy's owner was standing with two police officers. A police car was parked a few yards away.

"Thank goodness you're all right!" Happy's owner said.

KC smiled at the woman. "Thank you so much! We would have been trapped in that crypt forever if your dog hadn't found us!"

Marshall got on his knees and gave Happy a big hug. Happy licked Marshall's face and wiggled all over.

"Who locked you kids in there?" the male officer asked. He was a tall man with a friendly face.

"Leonard Fisher," KC said. "We have to hurry! He's getting away!"

"Leonard Fisher?" the officer repeated. "Isn't he the heir to the Smithsonian fortune?"

"Yeah," said Marshall, still holding Happy. "But he's not really an heir!"

KC quickly explained how Leonard Fisher had lied about being related to James Smithson.

"He put his great-great-grandfather's skeleton in the Smithsonian," Marshall added. "Then he stole James Smithson's skeleton and brought it here!" Marshall pointed through the door at the instrument case.

All three adults stared down into the crypt. The bones were easy to see in the sunlight.

"This is a crime scene," the female officer said. She walked to the cruiser and came back with a roll of wide yellow plastic tape. She and her partner quickly wrapped the tape around the crypt.

"Okay, let's go," the male officer said. "Where do you kids live?"

"We're not going home yet," KC told the man.

He looked at her. "So where do you want us to take you?"

"To the White House!" KC said.

Less than an hour later, the kids were sitting across from President Thornton, Vice President Kincaid, and KC's mom. The adults listened wide-eyed as KC told the story.

The kind police officers had called the

White House from their car. They'd been put right through to the vice president. She'd told the president, he'd called KC's mom, and all three had been waiting when the police car arrived.

Now they were in the president's private rooms. A maid had brought in sandwiches and they were all eating lunch. George the cat lay snoozing in a patch of sunshine.

"You went to Maryland on a bus without telling me?" KC's mom said. "If I weren't so relieved, I'd ground you right now!"

"I'm sorry, Mom," KC said. "But we had to follow Leonard Fisher. I just knew there was something weird about him."

"Well, as it turns out, you were right on the money," President Thornton said. He tapped a memo he was holding. "Our FBI agents picked up Mr. Fisher. He admitted everything."

"His idea was very clever," the vice president said. "Fisher assumed that we'd end up comparing his DNA with that of James Smithson. So he simply switched skeletons ahead of time. He never even told his lawyer what he'd done."

"He broke the air-conditioning in the Smithsonian," Marshall said. "Then he pretended to be a repairman so he could go in and swap the skeletons."

The president smiled at Marshall. "When you brought up DNA, Fisher was actually relieved," he said. "He couldn't suggest DNA himself or it would seem suspicious. So he was happy when you did it for him."

"What made you suspect him to begin with?" KC's mom asked.

KC pointed to the vase of tall flowers on the table. "When he came here, he was sneezing and told us he was allergic to lilies," she said. "But there weren't any lilies in the vase!"

"So Fisher wasn't a landscape designer for the rich?" the president said. "I wonder why he lied about that."

"I don't think he wanted you to know he worked for the cemetery," KC said. "He was afraid you'd find out his relatives were buried there and you might figure out his plan."

Mary Kincaid nodded. "I think you're right," she said. "Let's just all be grateful to that little dog."

The president glanced at KC and

Marshall. "I don't know why we need a police force or FBI agents," he said. "With you two on the job, crooks don't stand a chance!"

KC and Marshall blushed.

"Well, I have to get busy," the vice president said. "We have to return the two skeletons to their rightful resting places."

"And I have to get back to my office," KC's mom said, glancing at the president.

President Thornton stood up. "Yes, let me get a car for you, Lois," he said. "I'll call from the other room."

The president and KC's mom left the room together. KC and Marshall were alone with George the cat.

"Gee, that's funny," Marshall said as he reached for a cookie.

"What is?" KC asked.

Marshall grinned at KC. "I wonder why the president had to leave the room to use the phone? There's one right there on that table."

KC couldn't think of a good reason.

"I think they wanted to be alone," Marshall whispered.

"And I think *you* have an overactive imagination!" KC shot back.

"Me? That's the best joke I've heard in a year!"

Just then the door opened. The president and KC's mom walked back in.

"Are you two finished with lunch?" KC's mom asked the kids. "The car is ready for us."

As KC and Marshall got ready to leave, KC stole a glance at her mom and the president. They were standing next to each other by the door. The president's left arm and her mom's right arm were an inch apart.

But their pinkie fingers were touching.

The next day, KC and Marshall stood with the president in the Smithsonian Castle. The same two scientists as before removed the lids from the sarcophagus and a special container holding Smithson's remains. The scientists silently exchanged the two skeletons and replaced the lids. They left the building carrying old Mr. Fisher's skeleton in the container. They told the president they were on their way to Bowie, Maryland.

When the kids followed the president out of the Castle, KC was surprised to find her mom waiting on the steps.

"Mom, what're you doing here?" KC asked.

"I decided to take the day off," her mom said, glancing at the president.

"And I'm taking us all to lunch," the president said. "Your mother and I have something to tell you, KC."

Marshall snorted and gave KC a playful shove. He waggled his eyebrows.

KC returned the shove. She smiled at her mother and the president. "Good," she said. "I love surprises!"

Read KC and Marshall's next adventure!

The Spy in the White House

When KC and Marshall walked into the president's rooms, they got a shock.

KC's mom was crying. The president stood next to her, holding a newspaper in his hand.

"Mom, what's wrong?" KC asked. She hurried over to her mother.

The president held out the paper so KC and Marshall could see Darla Darling's column. The headline was at least five inches tall. It said:

PRESIDENT MAY
CANCEL WEDDING!

"Someone is spying on us!" Lois said, wiping her eyes. "They're hearing our private conversations!"

Did you know?

The SMITHSONIAN takes its name from James Smithson. He died in 1829 and left his money to a nephew. But when the nephew died with no children, all that money came to the United States—more than half a million dollars!

Why did Smithson leave his wealth to the United States? This has always been a mystery. He was born in France, grew up in England, and died in Italy. He never actually visited this country!

James Smithson was born into a wealthy family. When he grew up, he became a scientist and studied chemistry and geology. There's even a rock named after him—smithsonite.

We may never know why Smithson chose the United States to receive his fortune. But he wrote that he wanted the money to be used to create a place

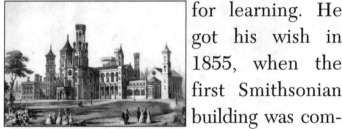

for learning. He got his wish in 1855, when the first Smithsonian building was completed. It was built of red stone and looked like a castle.

When James Smithson died in Italy in 1829, he was buried there. But in 1904, the United States sent Alexander Graham Bell to Italy to bring the remains to Washington, D.C. James Smithson would be pleased to know his final resting place is inside the first Smithsonian building.

About the Author

Ron Roy is the author of more than fifty books for children, including the bestselling A to Z Mysteries® and the brand-new Capital Mysteries series. He lives in an old farmhouse in Connecticut with his dog, Pal. When he's not writing about his favorite kids in Green Lawn, Connecticut, and Washington, D.C., Ron spends time restoring his house, gardening, and traveling all over the country.